Before I go on, just a *reminder* that if you see an **underlined word** anywhere, it means there's more info on it in the <u>Almanac</u> at the back of the book.

And just in case you haven't used your own Annoyingometer™ in a while, *I'll quickly remind you how it works.*

Once *activated*, the Annoyingometer™ senses things that will be annoying *to YOU*, in your *immediate* area.

I like to have mine set on 100 yards. If you set the distance too large, it will be picking up lots of *unnecessary* annoyingness.

The number scale goes from 0 to 127.

Unit	Comment
0	Nothing annoying anywhere near you
1-25	Barely Annoying
26-50	Sustainably annoying
51-75	Tolerable annoyingness
76-100	Starts getting uncomfortable
101-111	More uncomfortable—think about leaving the area
112-125	Very uncomfortable—leave the area immediately
126-127	Severely dangerous situation

Okay, so I'll
just strap
mine on.

What?!

Oh no, it looks like the
strap is broken!

I don't want to put it in my
backpack or pocket because
I need to be able to access
it quickly and *at* any time.

Hmmm, what to do?

Think, Dash, *think*...

Ah, okay, I have it!

This is going to be a
WORLD FIRST! You're quite
lucky to be witnessing this.

I'm going to **embed** the
Annoyingometer™ into
this actual book.

Readings will appear
automatically on the
top-right corner!

Okay, embed activated.

Enjoy the read.

Actually, whoops,
I forgot.

Some pre-reading
maintenance:

[1] Have you charged your
KB-15?

[2] Do you have
emergency snacks
available?

[3] Are you *comfortable?*

Okay, triple YES, great.
Time to read!

TOTAL MAYHEM BOOK 5
FRIDAY – THE TOTAL ICE CREAM
MELTDOWN

CONTENTS

Created by Ralph Lazar
Edited by Lisa Swerling

CHARACTERS

Friday –
The Total Ice Cream
Meltdown

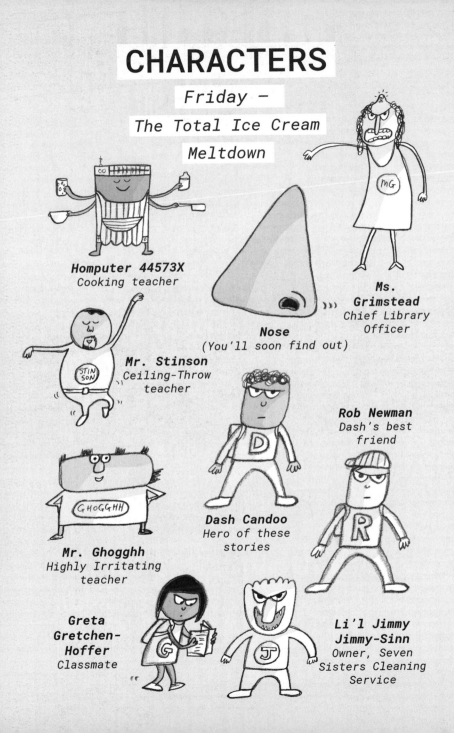

Homputer 44573X
Cooking teacher

Ms. Grimstead
Chief Library Officer

Nose
(You'll soon find out)

Mr. Stinson
Ceiling-Throw teacher

Rob Newman
Dash's best friend

Mr. Ghogghh
Highly Irritating teacher

Dash Candoo
Hero of these stories

Greta Gretchen-Hoffer
Classmate

Li'l Jimmy Jimmy-Sinn
Owner, Seven Sisters Cleaning Service

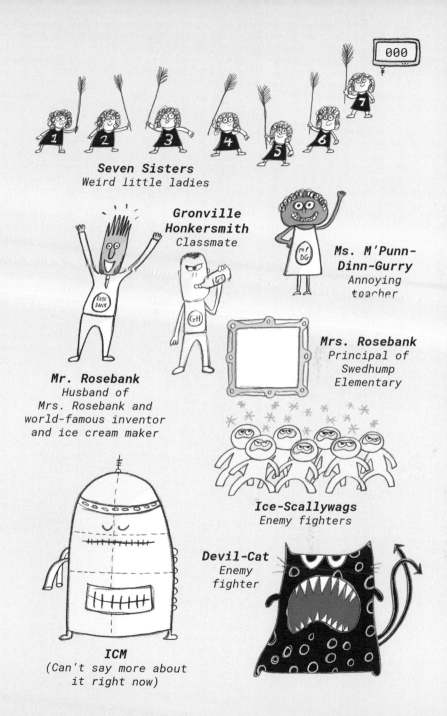

Seven Sisters
Weird little ladies

Gronville Honkersmith
Classmate

Ms. M'Punn-Dinn-Gurry
Annoying teacher

Mr. Rosebank
Husband of Mrs. Rosebank and world-famous inventor and ice cream maker

Mrs. Rosebank
Principal of Swedhump Elementary

Ice-Scallywags
Enemy fighters

Devil-Cat
Enemy fighter

ICM
(Can't say more about it right now)

Chapter 1
Before Breakfast

It really annoys me when
one gets into a
Total Mayhem Situation
before breakfast.

Which is **almost** what
happened to me this
morning.

On Fridays I tend to have
<u>deggs</u> for breakfast.
As you know, there are
four main types of deggs:

**[1] Fry
deggs**

**[2] Scramble
deggs**

**[3] Poach
deggs**

**[4] Boil
deggs**

Of these, **fry deggs** are
my favorite.

You?

Anyway, I had just sat
down to a plate of deggs
and a glass of fresh
<u>swamp juice</u>...

...when my **KB-15** started
flashing red.

Danger was close!

Before I had time to do
anything, the freezer
door burst open.

Inside I could see
SEVEN <u>scallywags</u>.

And they weren't just *any old scallywags*, they were

Ice-Scallywags!

This was serious.

Ice-Scallywags are small, but very, very, **very**, very, very, very, very, VERY, very, very, **very**, very, very, very, very, very, very, very, very, very, very, very, very, very, very, very, *very,*

very dangerous.

(And when something gets 28 verys from me, you know it's serious. And there are 28 verys. Count yourself if you don't believe me.)

I could say
I froze in shock.

But luckily I won't.

Because luckily
I didn't.

With lightning-quick
speed I deployed
Move #334
(**Freezer-Door-Slam**).

I grabbed a roll of
<u>concrete-tape</u> and quickly
taped up the freezer door
to stop them from coming
out again.

That was close!

I'd have to deal with
them *later*.

Then I heard
a noise.

A *weird shuffling,
sniffing, snuffling* noise
at the door.

*I braced myself for
another attack.*

More shuffling and
sniffing and snuffling.

And then in it came.

It looked like...

...a nose!!?

A huge nose, but not
attached to anything.

It didn't look *dangerous*,
just **ridiculous**.

And possibly *annoying*.

The nose came in and
started sniffing around
the kitchen.

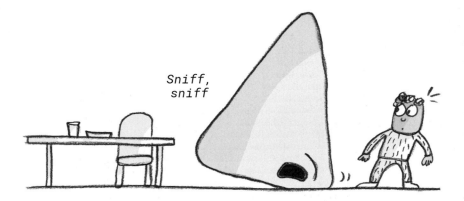

*Sniff,
sniff*

I moved to the side.

And it followed.

*Sniff,
sniff*

Uh-oh, watch the Annoyingometer™!

Enough of this nonsense!

I grabbed my breakfast
and ran outside.

The nose followed.

*Sniff,
sniff*

I quickly scaled a tree.

The nose came to the base of the tree and then started circling it, sniffing around and around and around.

But luckily it couldn't climb.

Sniff, sniff

Phew.

It sniffed around for a
bit more and then went
snuffling off.

That was weird.

Very weird.

Very, *very* weird.

But peace at last.

I ate my breakfast.

My deggs were cold, but
better than nothing.

Normally I'd be pretty
annoyed at stuff like
this before school.

But today was different.

Today was **FRIDAY!**

And Fridays are good.

After breakfast I climbed
down from the tree,
checked the concrete-tape
on the fridge *(still
secure)*, got changed, and
headed off to my school,
<u>Swedhump Elementary</u>.

Being a *Friday*, today
we'd be having an

end-of-day treat!

Always a good thing.

Just outside the gate,
I met up with my two
closest friends,
Rob and Greta.

Then off to morning
assembly we went.

Mrs. Rosebank, our school principal, who as you know is *totally invisible*, announced that today's treat would be

ice cream!

This is Henry, our school's <u>staircase moose</u>, in case you were wondering.

And not just
any old
ice cream.

It would be made by her
husband, **Mr. Rosebank**,
a **world-famous** *inventor*
and *ice cream maker*.

Instead of having
Library, usually our
first class on a Friday,
Mr. Rosebank was going to
show us all how his
impossibly exciting
Ice Cream Machine (ICM)
worked.

Ms. Grimstead, our Chief Library
Officer, **was not happy**.

Not happy at all.

Obviously,
her lump
started
throbbing.

But then when she heard
that Library class had just
been **rescheduled** to the
last period of the day,
she calmed down a bit.

The lump calmed down
a bit too.

Then off to the Ice Cream
Machine hangar we dashed.

The Ice Cream Machine was **ENORMOUS!**

Mr. Rosebank proudly told
us that it had taken him
fifty years to build.

He'd made the prototype (a baby ICM!) when he was in *elementary school*, winning first prize in the school science competition.

In *middle school* he'd
upgraded it, and by the
time he was a junior, the
ICM was a **fully-functioning**
device making over 100
ice creams a day.

Mr. Rosebank showed us all
the knobs and buttons and
pipes and <u>ossicles</u>.

The ICM was so complicated
that it *almost* seemed to
be a **LIVING CREATURE**.

For today's *end-of-school batch*, he was putting in:

10 gallons of **osteop milk**,

11 gallons of **walrus milk**,

12 gallons of
wombat juice,

13 gallons of **choc-hotlitt**,

14 gallons of **snolly juice**,

15 liquefied **pizzups**, and

16 bowls of **snorridge**.

Oh, and

1,000 deggs

(raw).

As he was explaining how the ICM worked, out of the corner of my **ear** I suddenly noticed a *revving* sound coming from outside.

From the hangar door I could see a strange little van passing by.

Then it passed by AGAIN.

And AGAIN!

It was *circling* the hangar!

I quickly got out my
<u>Cranio-cam</u> and **zoomed** in.

I could clearly read the
name on the side of the
strange little van:

AND there was a
really weird *little*
man driving it.

As I watched, seven *weird little ladies* got out with *feather dusters*...

...and started cleaning
the outside of the
Ice Cream Machine hangar.

What the heggleswick?!

I decided to take a
Cranio-cam photo.

One never knows.

One just never knows...

Chapter 3
Annoying

Next up was
Annoying class with
Ms. M'Punn-Dinn-Gurry.

She was crowned **World's Most Annoying Person** (by GAMA — the *Global Annoyingness Measuring Authority*) back in 2007, which is why she was hired by the school.

Nobody knows what she had done to win it. And no one is brave enough to ask.*

But it must have been pretty effective.

*Especially not Mr. Darling, because he's totally terrified of her.

Today's lesson was
divided into
four <u>snodules</u>.

Snodule 1: *Sing a catchy
song so it gets stuck in
someone's head.*

Gronville started singing
happy birthday even
though it wasn't
anybody's birthday.

Snodule 2: Repeat everything someone says.

What is snodule 2 again?

What is snodule 2 again?

What?

What?

Stop doing that!

Stop doing that!

Happy birthday to you, happy birthday...

In addition to this annoying conversation, the happy birthday song was now stuck in my head.

Snodule 3: *Stand over someone's shoulder while they're reading.*

SO annoying.

Snodule 4: *Ask LOTS of questions.*

How long is this class?

What is snodule 4 again?

What's the time?

Happy birth-day to whom?

What is that?

What was that?

Who is that?

I kept looking out the window at the ICM hanger, hoping to catch a glimpse of the suspicious van.

Rob and Greta did the same.

Ms. M'Punn-Dinn-Gurry suddenly stopped the lesson and looked at us.

"Staring out the window while I'm trying to teach is REALLY annoying!" she said.

Was this a good thing or were we in trouble?

She said the three of us
would have to go to
Mr. Ghogghh's room for
the next lesson, for some
specialist training in
how to be

Highly Irritating.

We had no idea what this
meant. She looked kind of
impressed with us, so we
guessed we were in some
kind of *good trouble.*

Then we heard ice cream.

...I mean,
a scream.

We looked out the window to see Mr. Rosebank **shrieking, flapping his arms** like a penguin at a *highly competitive flipper-flapping competition*, and running in small circles (*like a nose around a tree*) at the entrance to the Ice Cream Machine hangar.

"MY ICM HAS BEEN STOLEN! **MY ICM HAS BEEN STOLEN!**"

We **sprinted** outside just in time to see the strange little van driving off speedily *into the distance*.

And then it was gone.

"They must have shrunk it to get it in the van!" he yelled.

"Not good.
Not good at all.
Extremely dangerous!
Extremely dangerous to
shrink a machine like
that!" he added, with a
very, very, very, very
worried expression
on his face.

Once we had calmed
Mr. Rosebank down,
I printed out a photo of
the van and its driver
and gave it to him.

(I keep a <u>VVS-printer</u>*
in my backpack for
exactly *this purpose.)*

*Very-Very-Small

"Do you have an
Earlobe Transponder?"
Mr. Rosebank asked.

"Yes, an <u>ELT34!</u>" I replied.

"Excellent, put it on!" he said.

Then he ran off to his shed
to analyze the image.

I clipped on my ELT34.

Our **Highly Irritating** class
was about to begin.

So off we went to
Highly Irritating class
(which *obviously* was in the
Highly Irritating
building), unsure whether
to be **excited** or **worried**.

This is where we
were going, in case
you were wondering. →

HIGHLY
IRRITATING

MODERATELY
IRRITATING

IRRITATING

When we got to the
building, we were
surprised to see
that the door was
too high up
to open.

078

ENTRANCE

o

I love climbing things, but this was *definitely* irritating.

Once inside, the signposting was *impossible*. We had **no idea** which floor to go to.

Not good. I don't like being late for class.

Eventually we found the
elevator.

Rob pressed the **up** button
and we waited.

After five minutes we realized
while the button was real,
the elevator wasn't.
The doors were just painted
onto the wall!

Totally irritating.

Finally we found a *staircase*, and all I can say is they were **the** most irritating stairs we had ever walked up.

Eventually we got to
Mr. Ghogghh's classroom.

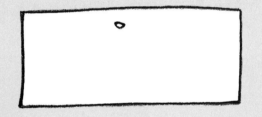

Mr. Ghogghh was very
impressed that we had
been sent to him.

"You must have done
something **really**
annoying!" he said.

"Before class starts,"
he said, "would you like to see
my marble run?"

Um, sure... Why not?

Mr. Ghogghh explained that he
was the **World Marble Run Champion
in 2017,** and after he won the
prize, he talked about it **so
much** and irritated everyone **so
much** that Mrs. Rosebank hired
him to come teach **Highly
Irritating** class at Swedhump
Elementary.

We admired his marble run.

It certainly *was* impressive.

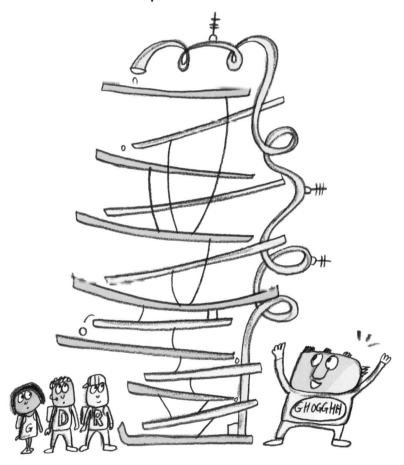

Then he started telling us all about it.

Well, the first section is modulated by a dual reticulated sprocket valve that gives the platform both elasticity and rigidity, allowing for a speedy launch of the marbles at the initial stages of the trajectory. Lower down I have recalibrated the sprocket valves to allow for heteroskedasticity and homoskedasticity, which allows for reduced spin and an increased glockenspiel quotient, which, as you well know, is fundamental to an effective beta-trajectory.

It soon got
mildly irritating,

then
moderately irritating,

and then
VERY irritating.

Mr. Ghogghh could see we were getting irritated, so he smiled.

And then he said, *"**NOW** I'm going to teach you how to be irritating."*

What?

We thought the marble run story **WAS** the lesson!

Then he looked at us and said:

Crocodile.

GHOGGHH

We looked puzzled.

Then he said it again.

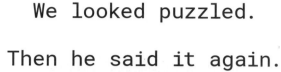

Crocodile.

Then again.

Crocodile.

GHOGGHH

Then he said:

Then:

Then:

Crocodile,
crocodile, crocodile,
crocodile, crocodile,
crocodile, crocodile,
crocodile, crocodile,
crocodile, crocodile,
crocodile, crocodile,
crocodile, crocodile,
crocodile, crocodile,
crocodile, crocodile,
crocodile.

Then:

"Crocodile, crocodile, crocodile, crocodile, crocodile, crocodile, crocodile, crocodile, *crocodile*, crocodile, *crocodile*, crocodile, crocodile, crocodile, crocodile,

crocodile, crocodile, crocod: dile, crocodile, crocodile, c *crocodile*, crocodile, crocodile, crocodile, crocodile, *crocodile*, crocodile, crocodile, crocodile,

crocodile, crocodile, crocodile dile, *crocodile*, crocodile, c crocodile, crocodile, crocodile, **crocodile**, crocodile, crocodile,

crocodile, crocodile, crocodile, cr crocodile, crocodile, crocodile, crocodile, crocodile, crocodil

rocodile, *crocodile*, crocodile,
rocodile, **crocodile**, crocodile,
ocodile, crocodile, crocodile,
rocodile, *crocodile*, crocodile,
rocodile, crocodile, crocodile,
, crocodile, crocodile, croco-
odile, crocodile, crocodile,
codile, *crocodile*, crocodile,
ocodile, crocodile, **crocodile**,
rocodile, crocodile, crocodile,
crocodile, crocodile, croco-
odile, crocodile, crocodile,
rocodile, **crocodile**, crocodile,
rocodile, crocodile, crocodile,
dile, crocodile, crocodile,
rocodile, crocodile, crocodile,
crocodile, crocodile, crocodile."

There are 100 crocodiles on this page. You are not allowed to continue reading the book unless you read each one out loud. Sorry. **Rule 27b**.

By now we realized what
was happening.

This was fast becoming a
Highly Irritating Situation.

On and on and on he went.

Greta went *GREEN*.
Rob went *RED*.
I started going
DANDELION.*

**That is a color, in case
you were wondering.*

Just as we all felt our
brains were about to turn
to *mush-slime* and seep out
through our earholes,
my **ELT34 buzzed.**

It was Mr. Rosebank.

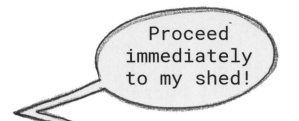

Proceed
immediately
to my shed!

he said.

But we were trapped in
a sea of crocodiles.

I pulled out my
Slow-Motion-ifyer, which
slowed the crocodiles down
to cccccccrrrrrrr-
rooooooooooocooooooood-
diiiiiiiiiiiiiiillllllllle,
giving us a way to escape.

There was **no way** we were going to try to **walk** out of this **idiotic building,** so we parachuted out!

Of course Mr. Ghogghh didn't even notice, as he was trapped in his slow-motion world.

As we floated, I realized how excited I was, for four reasons:

[1] because no kids at the school are ever-under-any-circumstances-ever ever allowed anywhere near or even **fairly near** or even *remotely near* Mr. Rosebank's shed,

[2] because he'd discovered something about the photo, I assumed,

[3] I can't remember what [3] was, and,

[4] because we had escaped temporarily from the crocodile earhole infestation.

The parachutes
auto-folded into our
backpacks...

...and we approached the shed.

But Mr. Rosebank had run to meet us outside.

Very disappointing. I really would **LOVE** to see inside that shed one day.

Mr. Rosebank had what looked like an old book with him.

"This is my elementary school **yearbook** from many years ago!" he exclaimed.

And then he opened it to show us a page inside.

Right there in the top corner
was a **YOUNG VERSION** of the
weird little man we'd seen in
the van.

"The van driver!" I exclaimed.

"That's Li'l Jimmy Jimmy-Sinn!"
Mr. Rosebank told us.

He sighed.
"We were *best friends*..."

"But not after I won
the school science
competition. *He's been
jealous ever since.*"

"And he's just **stolen** your
Ice Cream Machine!"
I concluded.

"A Friday without an
end-of-school treat is not
a *real* Friday!" said Rob.

And we all agreed.

"The weird thing is,"
said Mr. Rosebank,
"I know where he lives!"

"How?" we all asked
at the same time.

"He still lives in the
house he grew up in."

"Where?" we all asked at
the same time.

"In the **castle** out on *Misty Cliffs*," said Mr. Rosebank.

That was where he **lived**?

We couldn't believe it.

Misty Cliffs is a *CREEPY place*.

A VERY creepy place.

"I think we need to pay
him a visit!" I said.

Rob and Greta agreed.

**"But you have to be
careful,"** said
Mr. Rosebank. "He's little
but *highly* dangerous.
Good luck to
you all!"

We ran back to Highly Irritating class (*this time we knew the way!*) and got there **just as** the bell rang.

I clicked the Slow-Motion-ifyer off and the last cccccrrrrrrr-rooooooooooouuouuoonood-diiiiiiiiiiiiiiillllllle turned into a normal

crocodile.

GH OGGHH

"**And that is the end of the lesson!**" declared Mr. Ghogghh, without even having noticed our absence.

Chapter 5
Cooking

Would you rather
take a shower or
shake a tower?

Our next class
was **Cooking** with
<u>Homputer 44573X</u>.

Homputer 44573X was one of the first <u>homputers</u> ever built, and it had analyzed *every* meal **ever eaten** in the history of meals on the planet. It could thus come up with recipes **sure** to be *delicious*.

This was why Mrs. Rosebank had hired it.

As we ran to class, our plan was taking shape.

Our plan was to have
a plan.

And that plan would have
sub-plans.

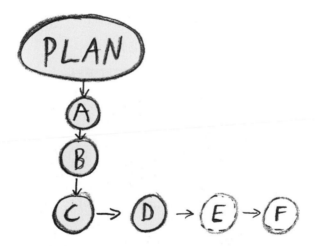

Sub-plan A, B, and C.
And *possibly* D if
necessary.
And *maybe* even E.
But *hopefully* **not** F.

Sub-plan A: As the class
was about to begin,
I would <u>warp-vortex</u> to
the castle, scope it out,
and then return. Greta
and Rob would stay
behind.

Then we'd formulate
Sub-plan B.

Everyone agreed.

Class was about to start.

Rob pulled out his
<u>Dublifier</u> and made a
clone of me to stay in
the cooking lesson.

VERY weird to see myself
from the *outside*. But no
time to dwell on that.

Homputer 44573X had already put on its apron and started taking out cooking implements and ingredients.

I removed the Warp-Vortex
from my backpack,

said the password
*(which I can't tell you,
so don't even ask)*, and
in a flash I was
sucked up...

...and deposited at the
castle entrance.

The gates were *quadruple-quadruple* bolted.

No point in even trying.

I deployed my <u>backpack-ladder</u>...

...and climbed up to the
window to look in.

Devil-Cat!

Clearly they were
planning something.

Something *bad*,
without a shadow
of a doubt.

But *where* was the
Ice Cream Machine?

I couldn't see it
anywhere.

So I returned to
my upward climb.

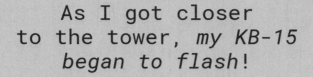

As I got closer
to the tower, *my KB-15
began to flash!*

I peered over the ramparts,
and then I saw them!

Zebra-hounds!

The tower was being
guarded by *zebra-hounds!*

They are **the worst!**
They are *beyond vicious.*

One would only have dogs
like that to guard
something precious.

Something *VERY precious.*

Like an
Ice Cream Machine!

Sub-plan A was complete.
Mission accomplished.

I was about to warp-vortex back to base when I noticed a weird tree stump next to the tower.

There was something familiar about it, even though it looked almost dead.

Then I saw it! A single leaf. It wasn't just *any* old tree.

It was a **Hammaphore Tree**!

Useful to know, Dash. Useful to know.

I *retracted* the
backpack-ladder,
activated the
Warp-Vortex, *said* the
password, and *whoosh*...

...I was back in Cooking
class.

And before me was a most
strange sight indeed!

Everyone was *lying on the floor* groaning, even my double.

They had cooked and eaten *such* delicious meals that **their stomachs could not quite believe it.**

I pulled out my own
Dublifier and quickly
de-doubled myself...

...and then lay there
myself, groaning so that
Homputer 44573X wouldn't
notice anything.

Then the bell rang.

So we all groaned out of there.

Being out in the sun seemed to help everyone's stomachs. I found the whole thing quite amusing and of course *couldn't miss an opportunity to laugh at Rob and Greta* for eating so much.

Our next class was **Ceiling-Throw** with **Mr. Stinson.**

On the way I told Greta
and Rob about Li'l Jimmy,
Devil-Cat, the tower,
the zebra-hounds, and the
Hammaphore Tree.

Greta immediately
pulled out her Almanac
and started reading
intensely.

Now for class.

Ceiling-Throw is a strange sport that Mr. Stinson himself invented. He is the **current World Champion.**

The first World Championships were held *last year*, and he was the only participant, but that is beside the point.

I have to say right now that it is **a very satisfying sport**, and I play it all the time.

This is how it works.

The player gets **object X**, throws it toward the ceiling, and then catches it when it comes down.

Object X is usually
something small and
soft like

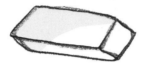

an eraser

a grape

a plum

a <u>heemo-globule</u>
<u>globule</u>

or anything else
similar in size.

The aim is to throw it **AS** **CLOSE AS POSSIBLE** to the ceiling **WITHOUT actually hitting** the ceiling.

*If you throw it too hard, it goes **thwump** and hits the ceiling.*

*If you throw it too softly, it **drops away** too soon.*

You need to get it
just right.

Gap of
0.5 mm

Niiiiice!

And when you do, it is
extremely satisfying.

Usually it takes three or
four or five throws to get
the hang of it.

I'd recommend trying it
at home.

In fact, I hereby grant
you permission to stop
reading this for five
minutes and give it a go
right now!

When Mr. Stinson won,
he actually used **HIS MOM**
as object X!

Gap of
0.3 mm

Niiiiice!

Official
Judge
Decider
Person

I **don't** recommend this.

Use something smaller
that won't damage the
ceiling or *hurt you* if
it lands on your head.

But we didn't have time
for this. We needed to
get to **Sub-plan B.**
And *fast*!

I took three *freeze-bombs*
out of my backpack and
gave one to Greta and one
to Rob.

We removed the pins
and threw them.

This **froze** the class and gave us *45 minutes* to get back to the castle to retrieve the Ice Cream Machine.

Mr. Stinson froze just as he was demonstrating his **pre-competition warm-up wiggle dance.** *It was quite an amusing sight.*

Greta told us that she'd read in the Almanac how to deal with zebra-hounds. They are **obsessed** with *Madagascar-pies*.

"And luckily," she said, "there is a fridge *full* of them in Cooking class."

So this was
Sub-plan B:

Rob and I would run past
Cooking class and grab
some Madagascar-pies.

Greta would fetch
Mr. Rosebank and
then go by
tunnel to the
*Secure Command
Center (SCC)* as
our backup team.

000

Rob and I would then:

[1] go to the Hammaphore Tree by Mrs. Rosebank's office,

[2] **enter the labyrinth,**

[3] get to the tower,

[4] **distract the zebra-hounds by feeding them Madagascar-pies, and then**

[5] climb into the tower to initiate **Sub-plan C.**

Sub-plan C was unknown at this stage.

So off we went.

First to get the pies, then up into the Hammaphore Tree...

PRINCIPAL ZO FIF

136

...and down into the
labyrinth.

In no time we emerged at the tower Hammaphore Tree.

Perfection!

Out we climbed and threw down the pies.

It worked!

The zebra-hounds were now
totally distracted.

I threw a <u>G-hook</u> to the window.

YES!
Bang on target!

I *pulled* it tight,
Rob *fastened* it to the
tree, and across
we shimmied.

Halfway across, Rob lost his hat. Luckily he always has a
backup hat in his backpack, known in some academic circles
as a Backup Backpack Hat. If the hat is black, it's known as
a Black Backup Backpack Hat. Perhaps one day there will be
an almanac for such a hat? It'll be a Black Backup
Backpack Hat Almanac. And that's that.

We climbed through the window and into the room.

We crept behind some boxes...

Happy birthday to you, happy birthday...

...and then we saw them:

The Ice-Scallywags!

First question:
How had they escaped
from the freezer?!!

And then we saw it!

One of them had a
holster, and in it
was an <u>MB44</u>, a device
specifically made
for cutting through
freezer doors!

Second question:
**What on earth were
they doing?**

And then we realized!

They were guarding the poor **shrunken** Ice Cream Machine, *encased* in a block of ice!

The scallywags hadn't seen us, which was a *good thing*.

But there didn't seem to be any way past them, which was a **bad thing**.

Using my ELT34, I buzzed Mr. Rosebank.

He was already in the SCC with Greta.

I (very quietly) told
them about the
Ice-Scallywags.

Greta looked in her
Almanac.

000

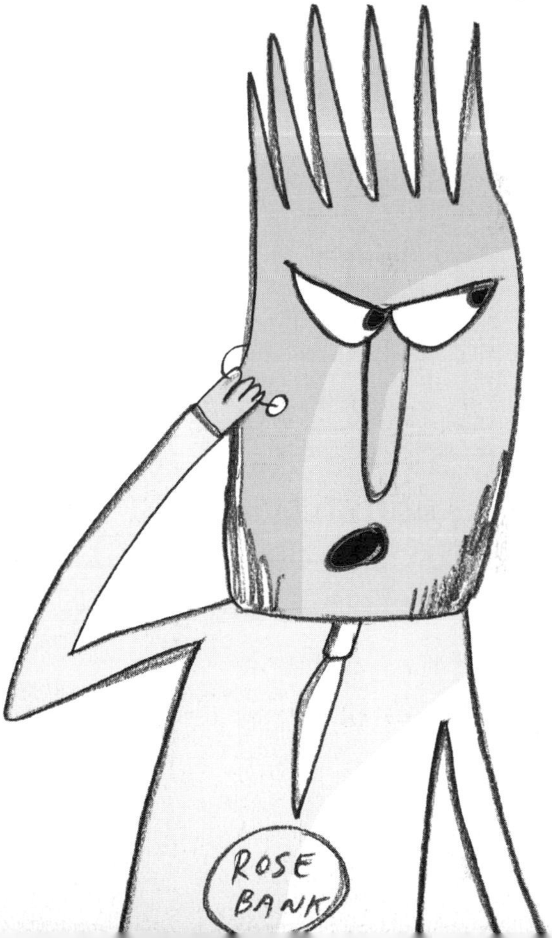
ROSE
BANK

But as he said that,
we suddenly felt an
intensely **cold chill**.

The Ice-Scallywags
were upon us!

Before we had time to do
anything, they deployed
Move #342
(**Instant Ice-Block**).

We were caught in a
BLOCK OF ICE!

Li'l Jimmy Jimmy-Sinn
and Devil-Cat appeared.

"So, Dash Candoo
and Rob Newman!" sneered
Li'l Jimmy Jimmy-Sinn.

"Or maybe Dash **Can-don't**
and Rob **OLD-man!**"
sniggered Devil-Cat.

"Ebenezer Rosebank thought he was *so* clever by winning the science competition all those years ago,

but I am cleverer!

"I have captured the ICM, and when I un-shrink it, I shall make the best ice creams in the world!

"I shall become rich, **VERY rich**, buy Swedhump Elementary, and then **FIRE** Mr. Rosebank and his invisible wife!

"Mwahahhahahhaha!

And maybe I'll turn the school into a parking lot, just for fun. *Such shall be my*

REVENGE!

"But in the meanwhile,
we'll be having a quick
meeting in my office.

"If you need anything,
just give us a shout!"

And with that, Li'l Jimmy,
Devil-Cat, and the scallywags
disappeared, leaving us
alone, *trapped*, and
very, very cold.

Meanwhile, back at school, Ceiling-Throw class was still frozen.

The bell rang for the next period. Greta and Mr. Rosebank were still in the SCC, so Greta simply *unfroze* the class using a *high-frequency* _defrost-ping_.

Everyone jumped up and
ran for the door while
Mr. Stinson carried on
with his *pre-competition
warm-up wiggle dance.*

Chapter 7
Library
Again

000

Ant #9,432, or his twin brother, ant #9,433, or their cousin Anton, ant #8,994, or Anton's sister, Antonella, ant #8,721?

157

Next up was meant to be
Library class.

But there was **no chance**
Dash, Greta, or I could
be there.

Drama was unfolding in the
tower **way too quickly** to
even *think* about the fact
that we were *missing* Library.

Greta and
Mr. Rosebank
warp-vortexed
directly
to us.

159

Despite the seriousness of the situation, Greta **actually started laughing** at us.

Then she used her <u>bear dryer</u>* to free us.

*A bear dryer is used to dry bears but can obviously also be used to melt ice.

When it was all melted,
Greta stood back and
asked,

"Why are you standing in
those weird positions?"

"Bbbbbbbecause
wwwwe're s-s-s-still
fffrrrrrozen!"

Feeling a little bad for
laughing at us, Greta
then pulled out her
Choc-Hotlitt Maker...

...and brewed us up a
quick cup. It worked
a treat!

Then, off to deal with
the enemy.

We snuck down to
Li'l Jimmy Jimmy-Sinn's
office.

And there they all were!

The seven scallywags,
Li'l Jimmy, and Devil-Cat,
all guarding the
shrunken, frozen ICM.

They were about
to un-shrink it!

Could we rescue the Ice
Cream Machine in time?

Devil-Cat
spotted us and **yelled**!

"Get them!"
shouted Li'l Jimmy.

The scallywags
immediately deployed
attack <u>Move #7,734</u>
(<u>Ox-Horn-Pincer</u>),
a very, very, very, **very**
dangerous formation.

Rob and I were about to deploy defensive **Move #8,001** (**Oscillating Nostril-Pump**), when Greta did something **TOTALLY** weird.

She pulled two huggy-bunnies out of her backpack and held them up high.

It was a *most strange* and, for some unknown reason, **terrifying sight.**

The scallywags' advance came to an **abrupt halt.**

Their **eyes widened...**

...and they **ran for their lives,** abandoning the Ice Cream Machine!

Turns out, as Greta explained, Ice-Scallywags are totally and completely terrified of huggy-bunnies.

Who would have known?!*

Someone had done her homework!

*Actually, you would have known had you read the Almanac.

As is well documented,
panic is contagious,
so Devil-Cat began to
freak out too, and then
to *run*.

And as you also know by
now, when he runs, **he RUNS**.
He was gone before you
could say Jonjon-
Jonjon-Jonjon Johnson!

Rob pulled out his <u>SPIN radio</u> to call for air support.

Within 27 seconds a
police <u>triplocopter</u>
swooped down and threw a
net of krypto-web over
Li'l Jimmy Jimmy-Sinn.

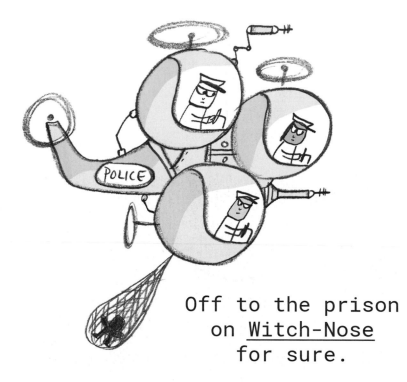

Off to the prison
on <u>Witch-Nose</u>
for sure.

All's well that
ends well...

...you'd think.

Rosebank then began to
shout:

"The ice is melting around
the Ice Cream Machine now
that the Ice-Scallywags
have gone!

"Because it's been SHRUNK,
it's **FULL of energy,** and if
it warms up too fast, **it
could be dangerous.**
We need to type in the
deactivation code,
and FAST!!!"

But it was **too late** –
the ice was melting *too
fast* for us to do anything!

The machine was warming up
faster than a <u>snodwidge pie</u>
in a <u>twoaster</u> in a desert!

The second the machine
became unfrozen,

KAZA-KAZABOOM

It turned into a monster!!

And it went *completely*

b'zonga!

We *ran* for cover.

Oh no! Looks like
Rob's about to
lose his hat
AGAIN.

The Ice Cream Machine started **blinking** and **snorting!**

Then *Total Rampage Condition* kicked in.

It **pulverized** the castle
and began *smashing*
trees and rocks and then
the entire hillside
while spewing out
thousands of ice creams.

TOTAL
MELTDOWN !

We had to act, and we had to act fast.

I pulled my ratchet-raptor from my backpack and activated it. Mr. Rosebank jumped on, **and up we flew.**

As we *swooped* over the monster, I *steered* the raptor into Inversion Mode 14c. Mr. Rosebank *leaned out* and attempted to type the **deactivation code** into the monster's control panel.

But it was **flailing** and
snorting, there were too
many flying ice creams, and
we just couldn't do it.

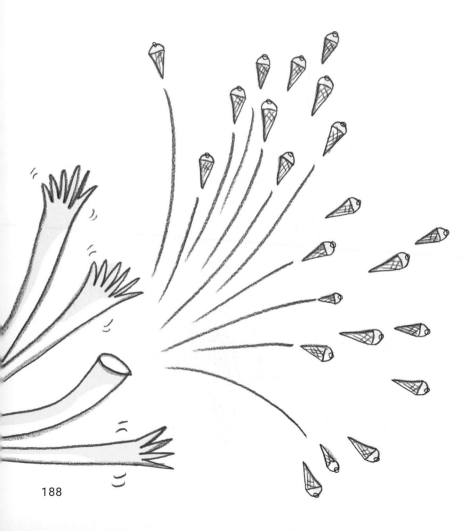

Again and again we tried.

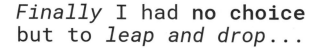

Finally I had **no choice**
but to *leap and drop*...

...and then *crawl down* to the panel.

Mr. Rosebank had
taken control of
the raptor and
yelled the code
down to me.

10810!

Success!

The monster was **deactivated** and now *began to shrink...*

...down to its original size and *temperament*.

As Mr. Rosebank landed,
it began to **whimper**.

But with some *soothing words* and a little *head scratch*, he managed to calm it down.

Rob, where's your hat?

Then together, **and much relieved**, we all walked back to school.

SWEDHUMP
ELEMENTARY

Ah, spare hat
in backpack!

Back at school, it turned out everyone had heard the *explosions* on the hill and Mrs. Rosebank had ordered everyone to **take shelter in the <u>Pickled-Cucumber building</u>** (which, as you know, is 100% earthquake proof).

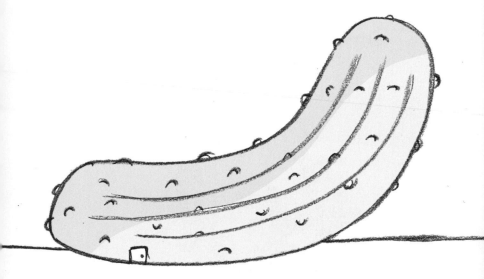

All classes were canceled.

Including Library,
yet again.

Mrs. Grimstead and her lump
normally would NOT be too
happy about this, but there
was something that was
cheering them up.

GRIM
STEAD

I'll give you a clue.

It begins with **ice** and
ends with **cream**.

Chapter 9
The End
of the Week!

Ant #66,253

The bell rang and now it
was **end-of-week
treat-fest.**

Mr. Rosebank *proudly* stood
at the control panel of the
Ice Cream Machine.

Mrs. Rosebank held his hand
(we think).

He tapped
the control
panel,

and whoosh!

All *was* good at
Swedhump Elementary.

Homputer 44573X

Mr. Ghogghh

Ms. M'Punn-
Dinn-Gurry

Mr. Grodzinsky

Mrs. Zhonst

Mr. Stinson

Mr. Proudfoot

Mr. Plumtree

Mr. Darling
and his pinkfish

Mr. Ibis

Mr. Hogsbottom

Mr. Steadyneck

Ms. Grimstead

Mrs. Belch-
Hick

Dog

208

All was good.

000

Happy birthday to you, happy birthday... ♪

Jeanjean-
Jeanjean-
Jeanjean
Johnson

Jonjon-
Jonjon-
Jonjon
Johnson

Collum Ollum

Ms. Ozniak

Mr. McYawn

Ms. Woodhouse

Dr. Williams

Mrs. Hogmanny-
Hog-Mahomm

Ms. Glissicle

Mr. Rrr-Tökk-Tökk

Mrs. Tadros

Mr. Nomsa-Nomsa-Nomsa

Myself!

Rob
Newman

Greta
Gretchen-
Hoffer

Gronville
Honkersmith

Ms. Greenacre
and Derek

The end.

Happy birthday to you, happy birthday...

Almanac

The COMPLETE ALMANAC is the place where you can find out everything about Dash and his world.
It's online here: total-mayhem.com/almanac
What you're reading now is the Book 5 Almanac, providing detailed information for this book only.

Annoyingometer™

An Annoyingometer™ is a wrist-mounted annoyingness detector. Range can extend up to 500 yards. Recommended range setting 100 yards and under. If you set the distance too large, it will pick up excessive annoyingness, which in itself would be annoying and might cause the device to malfunction.

The Annoyingometer™ is manufactured by Siena Industries Corporation. Ms. M'Punn-Dinn-Gurry and Mr. Ghogghh were involved with field-testing early models.

Similar devices include the Grumpometer™ and Sulkometer™. The broad spectrum Moodometer™, still in development and undergoing testing, is expected to be available in June next year.

The Annoyingness Measurement Scale (AMS) is calibrated globally, and all devices are rebooted and set to the new calibration every year on January 1. This means all devices work on the same measurement basis worldwide.

Calibration goes from 0 to 127.

0: Nothing annoying anywhere near you
1–25: Barely annoying
26–50: Sustainably annoying
51–75: Tolerable annoyingness
76–100: Starts getting uncomfortable
101–111: More uncomfortable — think about leaving the area
112–125: Very uncomfortable — leave the area immediately
126–127: Severely dangerous situation

Backpack-Ladder

A backpack-ladder (BPL) is an important piece of equipment used by Dash and Rob on multiple missions. While very useful, it can also cause injury if incorrectly deployed. Accordingly, it is very important to have clean airspace over you when deploying. No low-lying trees or low ceilings, and obviously don't deploy inside an airplane, train, hovercraft, or hot-air balloon. The same goes for *reverse deployment. Make sure there are no obstacles above you. When carrying one of these, make sure the top of your backpack is correctly fastened.*

In 2016, three employees at the BPL factory were injured during the testing process. The main backpack cover was not correctly fastened, and the ladder expanded inside the backpack, which then exploded. In 2019, a BPL auto-deployed in a factory staff member's car, causing him to drive off the road and into a shallow duck pond. Three ducks were injured and the factory had to pay a $25,000 fine. All three ducks recovered.

Bear Dryer
A bear dryer is like a hair dryer, but [a] it's huge and [b] it's used for drying bears instead of hairs.

If you have a wet bear, point the dryer toward it, turn the snozzle to setting 14, and activate. Either walk around the bear once every 30 seconds or ask the bear to do a slow, full rotation every 30 seconds, and it will be completely dry after four rotations. Also very useful for melting ice.

Ceiling-Throw
A strange and very satisfying sport that Mr. Stinson invented. The aim of the game is to throw an object (X) as close to the ceiling as possible without it touching. If you throw it too hard, it goes thwump and hits the ceiling. If you throw it too softly, it drops away too soon. Object X is usually something small like an eraser, an apricot, a marble, a heemo-globule globule, or anything else similar in size.

Choc-Hotlitt
Like hot chocolate, but better.

Hot Chocolate
Taste: 8.3/10
Flavor: 9.1/10
Smell: 7.5/10
Overall: 8.3/10

Choc-Hotlitt
Taste: 10/10
Flavor: 10/10
Smell: 10/10
Overall: 10/10

Code Beige
Part of the ELT34 international radio code.
Means "Hold your position, we are coming."
All ELT34 codes are listed in the ELT34 Manual.
Other examples of codes:
Code Maroon: "Dig a hole and hide in it!"
Code Mauve: "You can come out of the hole now!"
Code Avocado: "Would you like some guacamole?"

Concrete-Tape
Unbelievably strong (and expensive) tape
made of composite krypto-web fibers.
One strip is strong enough to support
a teenage osteop and someone the size
of Dash.

Cranio-Cam
Tiny, mind-activated camera embedded on the top of the
head. Dash and Rob each have one. These cameras are so
small that when unactivated they are almost invisible.
To activate a Cranio-cam, all you need to do is think about
it, and out it pops. Same goes for retraction. They're
waterproof and their batteries last forever.
Can only be embedded by registered
members of the CCEI (Cranio-cam
Embedding Institute). Photos and
films taken with them can be
tele-transferred to other
people who have Cranio-cams.

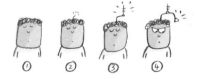

Defrost-Ping
This is a high-frequency radio beam that can defrost things
from a distance. For example, it can defrost a frozen chicken
from 3 miles away. The beams are not dangerous and can travel
through soil, rock, and concrete (except if the
concrete is reinforced with krypto-web fibers).

The Secure Command Center is equipped with one,
and its beams can comfortably defrost anything
on school premises.

Deggs

Deggs are eggs laid by Desert-Quails.
They are like chicken eggs but better.
They come in 132 different flavors.
Their flavor is activated by what kind of mood you're in,
and happens automatically.
For example, if you're in a bad mood, the degg will sense
that and become a flavor that cheers you up.
Main kinds are:

Fry Degg   Scramble Degg   Poach Degg   Boil Degg

Devil-Cat

Huge double-tailed black cat that always
lands on the wrong side of the law.
Tends to partner with criminals.
Fears nothing but fruit.
Terrified of watermelons.
However, he loves vegetables, especially
carrots.

Dublifier

This copies (or doubles) something if you zap it.
So for example, if you have just one slice of
pizzup but you want two, just zap it.

ELT34

An Ear-Lobe-Transponder-34 is an earlobe-mounted mind-activated
communications transponder. It operates
at a frequency of 34 Hector-Shnassils,
and comes in maximum pods of 12.
Typical use is in pairs or trios.
Example of paired use:
Person A and B each have one. If person
A wants to communicate with person B,
all he or she needs to do is think of person B and mumble a
prearranged password. This will immediately allow them to
communicate as if through walkie-talkies or a field radio.

Freeze-Bombs

As the name suggests, these weapons freeze everything
within 50 meters of the explosion. The effect lasts

exactly 15 minutes. They can be really
fun if you time them well. A freeze-
bomb explodes 2 seconds after it's been
thrown. If you try to time it just as
someone is pouring a glass of water or about to jump into
a pool, when the freeze effect wears off, it can be really
funny.

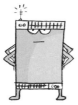

G-Hook
Invented by Greta Gretchen-Hoffer,
this is a throwable hook that will catch on almost
anything if thrown correctly. Super light and super
strong. Made of krypto-web fiber. Dash, Rob, and Greta
always have them in their backpacks.

Hammaphore Tree
Several Hammaphore Trees grow in the
forest next to Swedhump Elementary.
Each one is said to be over 500 years old.
Every Hammaphore Tree has a secret doorway
into a passage that connects to all other
Hammaphore Trees on the planet. Dash and Rob
are the only people who know this. Or so it's
believed.

SECRET
DOORWAY

Heemo-Globule Globules
These are small, very rare, highly precious globules
containing heemo-globules, which are mined all over
the world.

Homputer 44573X
Homputer 44573X is a homputer that specializes in
cooking. Its memory bank stores all recipes ever
made in the history of humankind. It also knows
all recipes that any human will prepare going
forward for the next 25 years. Teaches Cooking
class at Swedhump Elementary.

Homputers
Homputers are computers that can walk and have human-type
limb functioning.
They were invented by Mike Homputer in 1994.
Each has a serial number that denotes its specialty.

Examples:
44573X - Cooking
44573Y - Wobble-Ball
44573Z - Face-Pulling
44574A - Mailbox-Licking
44574B - Mailbox-Polishing
44574C - Whistling

Huggy-Bunnies

Huggy-bunnies are extremely cute bunnies that love
to be hugged. It is believed there might be something very dangerous about them, but to date,
we have not managed to discover what it is.
Ice-Scallywags are completely and utterly
terrified of them.

Ice-Scallywags

These are small, VERY dangerous scallywags.

How common: Rare
Special power: Can freeze anything just by standing near it
Weakness: Terrified of huggy bunnies
Typical group size: 7
Operate alone? Never
Maximum jump distance: 12 feet
Cleverness: 8/10
Speed: 9/10
Agility: 9/10

KB-15

Imminent Danger Warning Device (IDWD)

KB-15 Flash Codes:
* Red — on-off 1-second intervals
continuous: Imminent Danger
* Red — on 2s, off 2s: Imminent
lightning storm
* Green — on 3s, off 1s: Pizzup
delivery almost here
* Blue — on 5s, off 5s: Battery needs
charging

Madagascar-Pie

Very delicious pie loved by anyone who tastes it. Especially
loved by zebra-hounds.
Invented by Mrs. Nosey-Komba, who lives on a small island
off northern Madagascar. The recipe is actually classified

(i.e., top secret). Only people on the previously mentioned island know it. And, of course, Homputer 44573X, who knows every recipe ever invented.

MB44 (Freezer Door Cutter)
A device specifically made for cutting through freezer doors. Blades are made of razor-diamonds.

Move #334 (Freezer-Door-Slam)
Highly technical move used specifically to close freezer doors. Involves 4 steps:

[1] Launch   [2] Glide   [3] Kick   [4] Land

Left-footed and right-footed versions are taught in year-1 at Scallywag Academy.

Move #342 (Instant Ice-Block)
Terrifying and super fast specialty of Ice-Scallywags. Victims instantly get frozen in a block of ice and can't move.

They can, however, breathe. The ice lasts exactly 30 minutes. It's not actually dangerous to the victim but incredibly uncomfortable, inconvenient, and embarrassing.

Move #7,734 (Ox-Horn-Pincer)
Another Ice-Scallywag specialty. Involves formation of a C-shaped advance, i.e., a head with two horns that surround the enemy. Very dangerous. I repeat, very dangerous.

Move #8,001 (Oscillating Nostril-Pump)
Highly effective defensive move. Involves the rapid moving up and down of the elbows, to make the enemy believe they are being advanced upon by an oscillating nostril-pump. For

some reason, most scallywags are absolutely terrified of nostril-pumps. There is no known explanation why.

Nose

The part projecting above the mouth on the face of a person or animal. Usually.
Some noses are known to exist completely on their own, i.e., not attached to the face of a person or animal. Very few have been spotted.
Most noses contain the nostrils and are used for breathing and smelling.

Ossicles

Ossicles are small osculated sniccles containing micro-heemo-globule globules. They are used as conductors in

advanced electronic devices. They are extremely difficult to work with as they can be quite sticky. Only very advanced engineers and inventors use them.
Mrs. Tadros (the science teacher at Swedhump Elementary) has a fine collection of them.

Osteop Milk

It's pretty easy to milk osteops. Their milk tastes better if milked with the left hand.
Doctors recommend one glass daily, to be drunk between 7 a.m. and 8 a.m. If you drink it after 8 a.m., you might get an upset elbow.

Pickled-Cucumber Building

The walls of this building are 3 feet thick and made of solid cucumber (pickled) sponge. Accordingly, it can with-stand major explosive impact, intense pressure trauma, and high-magnitude vibrations. If there

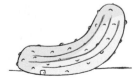

was going to be an earthquake, inside this building is where you'd want to be. The only downside is that after more than 15 minutes inside it, you will smell of pickled cucumber. The smell is actually not possible

to wash off. It only comes off with time. Usually
8-10 days.

Pizzup
Pizzup is like pizza but different. And better.
Not only because it tastes better, but because one of the
key ingredients is hover-yeast, which allows the pizzup to
levitate (or float). So it can hover above a surface.

For example, if your desk is covered in stuff, you can have a
pizzup without any problems, because it will hover above the
clutter. Or, if you're riding your quadcycle, you can get a
pizzup to fly alongside you for easy eating. They have been
known to hover at speeds in excess of 41 miles per hour.
Disappointingly, eating a pizzup doesn't have any effect on
your own gravitational pull. Collum Ollum once tested this
by eating a dozen pizzups. Big ones. It didn't make him
float but did make him vomit. Don't try it yourself.

Ratchet-Raptor
One- or 2-seater hover-bird. Highly mobile and can fly
fast. Can reach altitudes of 800 feet and has a cruising
speed of 80 mph. Battery last 3 hours in full flight mode.
Deployable in 3 seconds. Packable in 5 seconds. When packed,
it's about the size of a golf ball. Dash usually has one in
his backpack.

The first ever ratchet-raptor was test-piloted by James
Hogsbottom. On its maiden flight, the navigation nyeffy-gimble
was on the wrong setting (18 instead of 16) and he crashed into
an osteop shed on a neighboring farm. Luckily he wasn't
injured in the crash, but there were over 200 osteops
in the shed at the time, and they got such a fright
that they began a stampede. It's actually known in
the history books as the Great Osteop Stampede
of 2008. The osteops ran so far that a
squadron of police triplocopters
and triplo-triplocopters had to
retrieve them individually.

The farmer, a woman by the name of Jezebel-the-Magnificent, was initially going to sue Mr. Hogsbottom, but then she was interviewed on TV. She was so happy to have been on TV that she forgave him, and they are good friends to this day.

Rule 27b
The reader shall not be allowed to continue reading the book unless all words appearing on the page (on which Rule 27b occurs) are read out loud.

Scallywags
There are many different types of scallywag. Each type has its own fighting techniques, strengths, and weaknesses.

Secure Command Center (SCC)
The SCC is the technology headquarters for Dash and Rob. It's where their communications, surveillance, and airborne/waterborne reconnaissance hardware is stored and operated. It's only accessible by tunnel.

Slow-Motion-ifyer
A Slow-Motion-ifyer allows you to slow down everything around you, but not you yourself. So for example, if you are taking an exam and you need more time, you can just slow the whole room down and, voilà, take as long as you want.

Snolly Juice
Snolly juice is the perfect accompaniment to snorridge. Its name is actually an acronym for the ingredients.

SNO: Snow
L: Lemon juice
L: Linguini
Y: Yogurt

Snodules

Snodules are components of a technical class
or lesson. A typical lesson might have 4 or 5
snodules that are interrelated but also
independent. Snodules can be divided into
sub-snodules, semi-snodules, and snodulated-snodules.
Snodulated-snodules can be divided into sub-snodulated-
snodules, semi-snodulated-snodules, and snodulated-snodulated-
snodules. Snodulated-snodulated-snodules can be divided into
sub-snodulated-snodulated-snodules, semi-snodulated-snodulated-
snodules, and snodulated-snodulated-snodulated-snodules.

Snodwidge-pie

Totally delicious pies.
How to make them:
[1] Get a snod-hemple sandwich.
[2] Remove the hemple, and then the snod.
[3] Liquidize the snod and boil in walrus milk for a year.
[4] Add yeast and desiccated anchovy.
[5] Bake at a temperature of 325 degrees for 2 years.

Snorridge

Snorridge is like porridge, but better. It's like normal
porridge, but made with snow. If you don't live in a snowy
place, you can buy your own snorridge-snow-maker and have it
in the kitchen. If you do live in a snowy place, better to use
fresh snow.

Often accompanied by a glass of fresh snolly juice.

Most supermarkets stock snorridge, but demand would be so high
if it was on a normal shelf that it's usually tucked away on
a secret shelf. If you go to the cereal section in a regular
supermarket and stand right in the middle of the
display and then pull away the boxes at belly-button
level, usually that's where the secret shelf is located.

There are seven main flavors, each named after a day of the
week. If you eat the right one on the right day, it will be
delicious, but if you eat the wrong one, it will be awful.

Saturday snorridge on a Saturday is apparently the most

delicious, but Saturday snorridge on a Monday tastes particularly disgusting, and in some extreme cases might involve hospitalization.

SPIN Radio
A SPIN Radio (Secure Police Interface Neo-mogrifier) lets the user communicate directly with International Police Headquarters. Very few exist, and only highly trained experts are allowed to use them. It folds up to the size of a small pea. Rob Newman usually has one with him.

Staircase Moose
Friendly creatures that can be tamed and become very useful for assistance with reaching things. Same life span as humans. The staircase is not there when born and usually only starts growing once the moose reaches the teenage years. Large herds of them are found in the northern reaches of Moremi Forest.

Swamp juice
Swamp juice does not actually come from a swamp. Like many of Dash's breakfast beverages, its name is an acronym:

S: Swed milk
W: Wombat juice
A: Artichoke juice
M: Marzipan
P: Pickled cucumber

And yes, it's delicious.

Swedhump Elementary
Dash's school.
Principal: Mrs. Rosebank
Probably the best school in the world.
Definitely has the best teachers in the world.
Named after the hump of a swed, a two-faced humped creature.

Triplocopter

Triple helicopters invented by G. & J.
Tarrow Siblings Inc. in 2010. The equiva-
lent of three helicopters stuck together.
They are sixty-one times faster and seventeen
times more powerful than regular helicopters,
though more complicated to fly. The test pilot
of the first version was James Hogsbottom, who teaches Paper
Airplane class at Swedhump Elementary. There have been no
reported triplocopter crashes to date.

Twoaster

A twoaster is a toaster that takes 12 slices of bread.
The numbers on the eject dial refer
to height in meters. So if you set
it to 12, once done, the toast
will fly at least 12 meters
high. Can be useful in combat
situations.

VVS-Printer

A VVS-printer is a Very-Very-Small printer. Dash keeps one
in his backpack at all times. When in off-mode, it is the

size of a pea. When activated, it can enlarge to
the size of a regular printer. A VVS-printer comes
standard-issue with never-ending ink cartridges.

Walrus Milk

It's quite dangerous milking a walrus. But worth it,
because their milk is delicious. Dash has a distant
relative who is friendly with the brother of a man whose
best friend's sister's uncle's aunt's son's son has a
walrus farm, and so Dash is able to get supplies.

Warp-Vortex

A Warp-Vortex allows the warpee (owner) plus sub-warpee
(passenger) to move from one place to another in a trilli-
second. Warp-Vortexes are typically backpack-mounted.

Pocket versions do exist but are quite expensive.

Each Warp-Vortex has its own password, which the users will not share under any circumstances (so don't even ask).

Witch-Nose Island

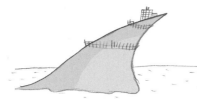

Witch-Nose Island is the most secure prison ever. The entire perimeter is ringed by 27 krypto-web fences, 11 of which are electrified. The water around it is freezing and full of shnarks (which are more vicious than sharks); flesh-eating, saw-toothed doublodiles; and killer electric rays. No prisoner has ever escaped from it.

Wombat Juice

Wombat juice actually has nothing to do with wombats.

The name comes from its ingredients:
Walrus milk
Octopus saliva
Mango
Beetroot
Avocado
Tomato

Blend them in any proportions, then serve with ice. Delicious!

Zebra-Hounds

Absolutely awful, terrible, horrible, vicious dogs.
Extremely expensive.
And extremely stupid.
Tend to be owned by criminals.
Favorite food: Madagascar-pie.

FOR DASH CANDOO, EVERY DAY IS...
TOTAL MAYHEM!

ABOUT THE CREATORS

Ralph Lazar and Lisa Swerling live in California.

Ralph made up the Dash stories (inspired by wrestling his godson — Dash!) and did the drawings. Lisa shaped the stories into this book.

Ralph and Lisa are the creators of the popular illustrated project Happiness Is..., *which has been translated into over twenty languages and has over three million followers online. They also wrote and illustrated the* New York Times *bestseller* Me Without You.

Their studio website is lastlemon.com

Ralph is also a painter, and Lisa makes miniature worlds in boxes.

Ralph's art website: ralphlazar.com

Lisa's art website: glasscathedrals.com